First published by Parragon
in 2007

Parragon
Queen Street House
4 Queen Street
Bath BA1 1HE, UK

ISBN 978-1-4054-9471-7
Printed in China

Little Pony's Secret

Illustrated by Sophie Groves   Written by Kath Smith

PaRragon

Bath New York Singapore Hong Kong Cologne Delhi Melbourne

Dizzy was a little wooden pony on a merry-go-round near the seashore. Every day, she and her friends gave rides to children as pretty music played.

Although she loved her job, Dizzy had a secret dream.

"I wish I could see the ocean," she sighed each night. She could hear the waves nearby, but she had never ever seen them.

But Dizzy's wooden hooves were stuck
firmly to the merry-go-round.

One night, when the children had gone home, Dizzy thought about being a real pony. "I wish I could gallop," she said out loud. Suddenly, a shooting star whizzed across the sky!

A wish made on a shooting star is very special. It is so special that it can come true...

All at once, Dizzy could toss her mane and swish her tail.
All at once, she could kick her hooves high in the air!

"I'm a real pony!" she cried, as she jumped off the merry-go-round.

"I'm free!" neighed Dizzy the little pony.

"I can go wherever I want!"

As Dizzy raced toward the beach, a beautiful white horse joined her. They galloped like the wind onto the soft sand.

Soon Dizzy and her new friend reached the water's edge.
"Let's gallop through the waves," neighed the white horse.

"The ocean is even more beautiful than I imagined," Dizzy neighed happily, as they splashed about in the sparkling surf.

"The world is full of beautiful things,"
said the white horse. "Come with me and
we can see them all."

Dizzy remembered her friends on the merry-go-round, and she remembered the children's smiles.

"Thank you, but I have an important job to do," she neighed, and off she galloped.

When the children came to the merry-go-round for a ride, Dizzy was there waiting for them.

"That's funny!" said a little boy, as he climbed on to her back.

"This pony is all wet, and there's sand everywhere. Where did it all come from?" he asked. But no one could guess. It was Dizzy the little pony's big secret!